Run to Win

Written by Samantha Montgomerie
Illustrated by Amy Zhing

Collins

Bang! They dash off.

Pip jogs.

Rex is quick.

He winks at Pip.

Will has a long neck.

Thud!

Pop! Jack sinks.

He is wet.

This mud is thick.

Pip winks at Rex.

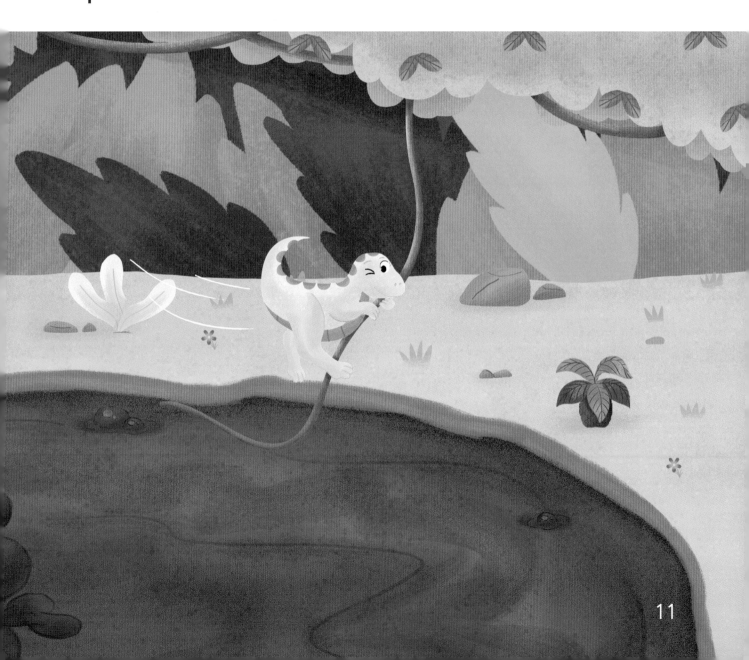

Pip can finish.

She runs to win.

15

After reading

Letters and Sounds: Phase 3

Word count: 40

Focus phonemes: /j/ /w/ /x/ /qu/ /sh/ /th/ /ng/ /nk/

Common exception words: they, he, she, to

Curriculum links: Personal, social and emotional development; Understanding the world

Early learning goals: Reading: read and understand simple sentences; use phonic knowledge to decode regular words and read them aloud accurately; read some common irregular words

Developing fluency

- Your child may enjoy hearing you read the book.
- Encourage your child to read the sounds with expression, and to use a humorous tone for this funny story.

Phonic practice

- Focus on words in which two letters together make one sound.
- Begin by pointing to **Bang!** on page 2. Say: N and g make one sound /ng/ so this word is: B/a/ng – Bang. Repeat for **dash**, saying: S and h make one sound /sh/ so this word is d/a/sh – dash.
- Take turns to point to a word for each other to read.
- Look at the "I spy sounds" pages (14–15) together. Take turns to find a word in the picture containing a /x/ or /th/ sound. Remind your child that it could be a name of a character. (e.g. *Rex, box, six; teeth, three, throw*)

Extending vocabulary

- On page 4, ask your child what word is the opposite of **quick**. (*slow*)
- Ask your child to suggest words or phrases with an opposite meaning to these:

  long (*short*)   wet (*dry*)   thick (*thin*)   win (*lose*)